Dear Parent:
Your child's love of reading starts here!

Every child learns to read in a different way and at his or her own speed. Some go back and forth between reading levels and read favorite books again and again. Others read through each level in order. You can help your young reader improve and become more confident by encouraging his or her own interests and abilities. From books your child reads with you to the first books he or she reads alone, there are I Can Read Books for every stage of reading:

SHARED READING
Basic language, word repetition, and whimsical illustrations, ideal for sharing with your emergent reader

BEGINNING READING
Short sentences, familiar words, and simple concepts for children eager to read on their own

READING WITH HELP
Engaging stories, longer sentences, and language play for developing readers

READING ALONE
Complex plots, challenging vocabulary, and high-interest topics for the independent reader

ADVANCED READING
Short paragraphs, chapters, and exciting themes for the perfect bridge to chapter books

I Can Read Books have introduced children to the joy of reading since 1957. Featuring award-winning authors and illustrators and a fabulous cast of beloved characters, I Can Read Books set the standard for beginning readers.

A lifetime of discovery begins with the magical words **"I Can Read!"**

Visit www.icanread.com for information on enriching your child's reading experience.

Spider-Man versus Venom
Copyright © 2011 Marvel Entertainment LLC and its subsidiaries. MARVEL, Spider-Sense, Spider-Man: ™ and © 2011 Marvel
Entertainment LLC and its subsidiaries. Licensed by Marvel Characters B.V. www.marvel.com. All rights reserved. Printed in the
United States of America. No part of this book may be used or reproduced in any manner whatsoever without written permission
except in the case of brief quotations embodied in critical articles and reviews. For information address HarperCollins Children's
Books, a division of HarperCollins Publishers, 10 East 53rd Street, New York, NY 10022.
www.icanread.com

Library of Congress catalog card number: 2010938192
ISBN 978-0-06-162630-2
Typography by Joe Merkel

11 12 13 14 15   LP/WOR   10 9 8 7 6 5 4 3 2 ❖   First Edition

SPIDER SENSE®
SPIDER-MAN

Spider-Man
versus Venom

by John Sazaklis
pictures by Andie Tong
colors by Jeremy Roberts

HARPER

An Imprint of HarperCollinsPublishers

PETER PARKER

Peter is a good student and a photographer. He also has a big secret: He is Spider-Man!

AUNT MAY

Peter lives with his aunt May. They take care of each other.

EDDIE BROCK

Eddie used to work at the *Daily Bugle* until his bad attitude got him fired.

SPIDER-MAN

As Spider-Man, Peter uses his superpowers to help people.

J. JONAH JAMESON

Mr. Jameson is Peter's boss at the *Daily Bugle*.

VENOM

This new villain in town has powers like Spider-Man, but he's here to cause trouble!

Peter Parker was enjoying his day off
at home with his aunt May.
"These pancakes look yummy,"
Peter said.

Suddenly, a news flash on TV
grabbed Peter's attention.
"A monster is attacking
the city!" said the reporter.
Peter jumped out of his seat.

"This is my chance

to impress my boss," Peter said.

"I've got to snap pictures!"

"Please take a snack," said Aunt May.

"And do be careful, Peter!"

Secretly, Peter changed

into Spider-Man!

He grabbed his camera and a banana,

and then he swung through the air.

"I feel like a spider monkey!" he said.

Across town, the monster climbed

to the top of the *Daily Bugle*'s building.

He was large and mean,

and had sharp teeth and claws.

He crashed through a window.

"I am VENOM!"
roared the monster.
"And I'm in charge now!"
J. Jonah Jameson was
shocked and scared.

Venom shot black webs
and tied Mr. Jameson to the wall.
"Who do you think you are?"
he yelled at Venom.

"You don't remember me?"

asked Venom.

He pulled off his mask.

The monster was really a man!

"Eddie Brock!"

shouted Mr. Jameson.

"That's right!" said Eddie.

"After you fired me

from the *Bugle*,

a slimy alien creature fell on me.

It attached itself to my body

and gave me superpowers.

Now I am Venom—

and I am out for revenge!"

Spider-Man followed the damage
to the *Daily Bugle* building.
He saw that Mr. Jameson
was in danger!

Spidey webbed his camera to the window,
and then he sprang into action.

"Stop the presses!" Spider-Man yelled.

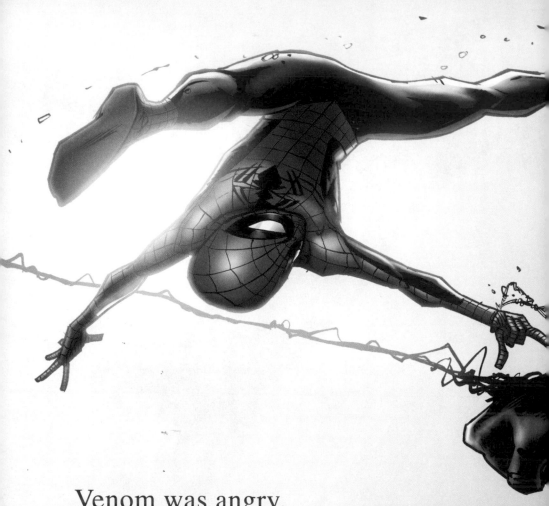

Venom was angry.

"Looks like we have a bug problem!"
he snarled.

Venom shot his webs at Spider-Man.

"Hey, those are *my* moves," said Spidey.

"Here's web in your eye!"

Spidey covered Venom's face.

The villain could not see.

Venom ripped off the webs and roared.

Spider-Man leaped onto the wall.

He tried to free Mr. Jameson,

but Venom grabbed him.

"My, what big teeth you have!"
Spider-Man said.

Venom had a strong grip,

but Spider-Man broke free.

Venom charged.

SMASH! CRASH!

The walls shook and cracked.

"I have to find a way
to stop that violent villain,"
said Spider-Man.

Venom ripped a heater from the wall
and aimed it at Spider-Man.
Suddenly, the pipes began
to blast hot steam.

The heat made the alien weak.

It could not stay on Eddie.

That gave Spider-Man an idea.

He shot a web at the pipes

and pulled them toward Venom.

The super-suit began to melt away.

Eddie became even angrier.

"You need to let off some steam,"
said Spider-Man.

Spider-Man pulled Eddie out of the suit and webbed him to the wall.

"Hang tight," Spider-Man said.

"The police will be here soon."

"Let's not forget about you, Slimy,"
Spidey said as he trapped the alien
inside a metal wastebasket.
He sealed it shut with extra webbing.
Then he helped free Mr. Jameson.

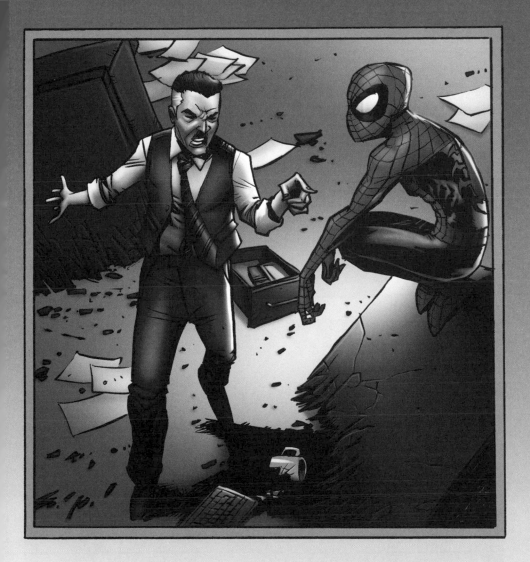

"Look what you did to my office,"
Mr. Jameson yelled. "It's a mess!"
"Now look who's hot under the collar,"
said Spider-Man.

The police arrived
and took Eddie to jail.
A scientist carried the alien
back to his lab to study it.

When no one was looking,

Spider-Man got his camera and left.

He had to develop his pictures quickly

and give them to Mr. Jameson.

Mr. Jameson liked the photos.

"Must be your lucky day, Parker.

These are going on the front page!"

Peter smiled to himself.

It was Spider-Man's lucky day, too.